DUSSEHRA

Om KIDZ
An imprint of Om Books International

Dussehra is an Indian festival celebrated every year with gaiety and grandeur. It falls in the Ashwin month of the Hindu calendar sometime between the end of September and October.

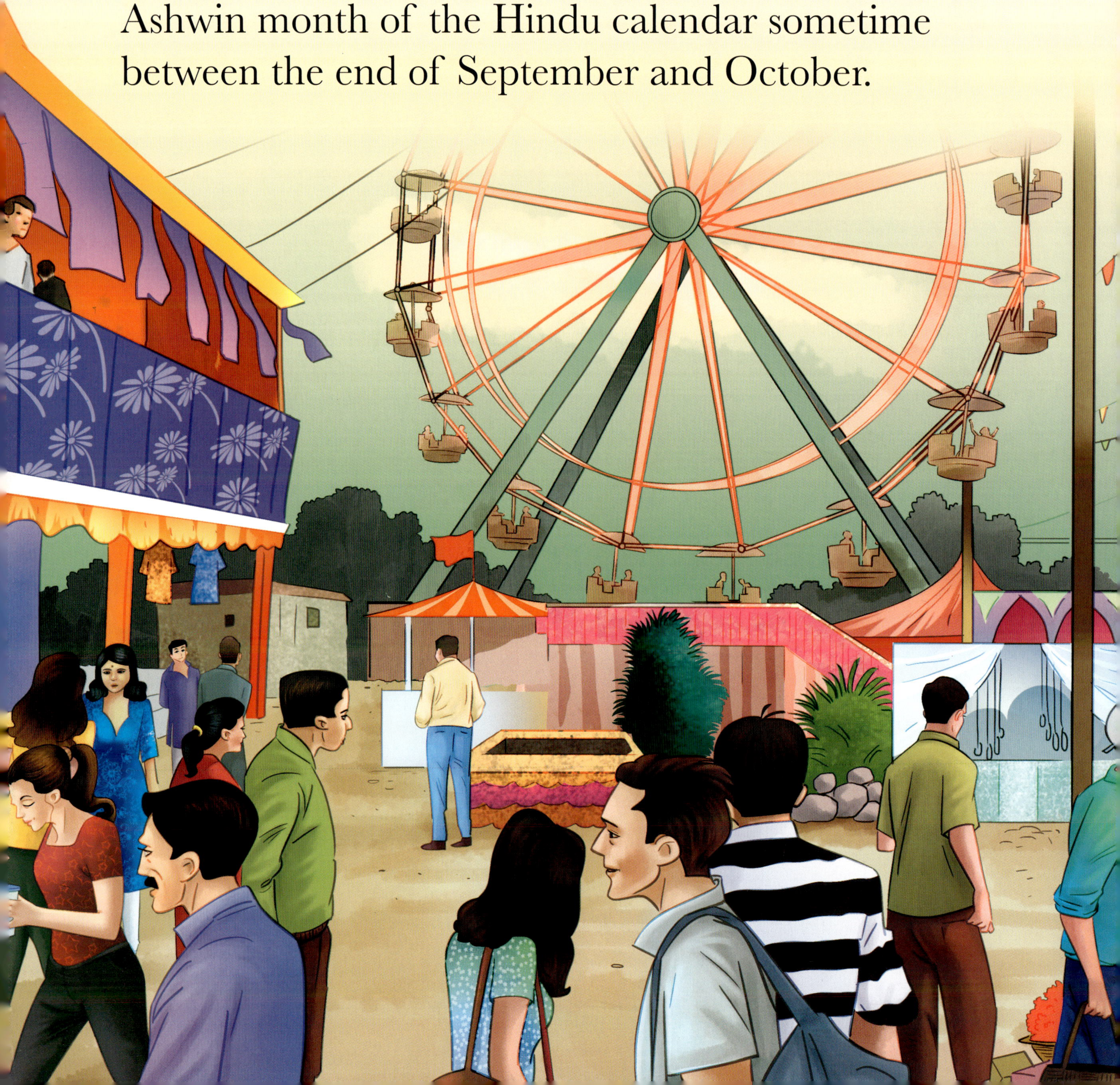

Also known as Vijayadashmi, Dussehra is celebrated to honour the triumph of good over evil. There are several mythological tales linked to this day of celebration.

According to the ancient Indian epic Ramayana, on this day Lord Rama, the seventh avatar of Vishnu, killed Ravana. Ravana was the ten-headed Demon King of Lanka. He abducted Sita, the wife of Lord Rama, to take revenge of the humiliation of his sister, Shurpanakha.

Ravana was very powerful and was said to have the nectar of immortality stored in his belly button. It is believed that before starting for his battle with Ravana, Lord Rama worshipped Goddess Durga who gave him the secret knowledge of how to kill Ravana.

Lord Rama rescued Sita after a ferocious battle with the help of Hanuman and the Vanar King Sugriva. Lord Rama defeated Ravana on the tenth day (Dashmi) of Ashwin month and achieved victory (Vijaya). Hence the day is also known as Vijayadashmi.

Lord Rama, along with Lakshmana, Sita and Hanuman, returned to Ayodhya twenty days after Dussehra. The people of Ayodhya celebrated their return by lighting earthen lamps. This day is celebrated as Diwali every year.

Another tale associated with Dussehra marks the victory of Goddess Durga over the evil buffalo demon Mahishasura after a battle that lasted for ten days and nine nights.

The nine days preceding Dussehra, also known as Navratra, combine the worship of the nine different forms of Goddess Durga as well as the spectacle of Ramlila - an enactment of the life of Lord Rama.

On Dussehra, the concluding day of Ramlila, actors enact the final important episodes of the battle. In the evening, huge effigies of Ravana, his brother Kumbhkarana and son Meghnadha, with crackers placed inside them, are burnt in vast open grounds.

After the final war with Ravana, the actor playing Rama shoots an arrow with a flaming tip at the effigies from a safe distance.

Celebrations are carried on in full swing in different parts of the country like 'Garba' in Gujarat and

playing of the 'Dhak' in West Bengal. In West Bengal, this festive period is celebrated as Durga Puja or Durgotsav. Grand fairs are also organised on this day.

The most famous Dussehra celebrations in India are those in the city of Mysore. The Mysore palace is illuminated with numerous lights during the festive period. Goddess Chamundeshwari is worshipped on this day and a grand procession of her idol (locally known as Jumboo Savari) is taken out across the city.

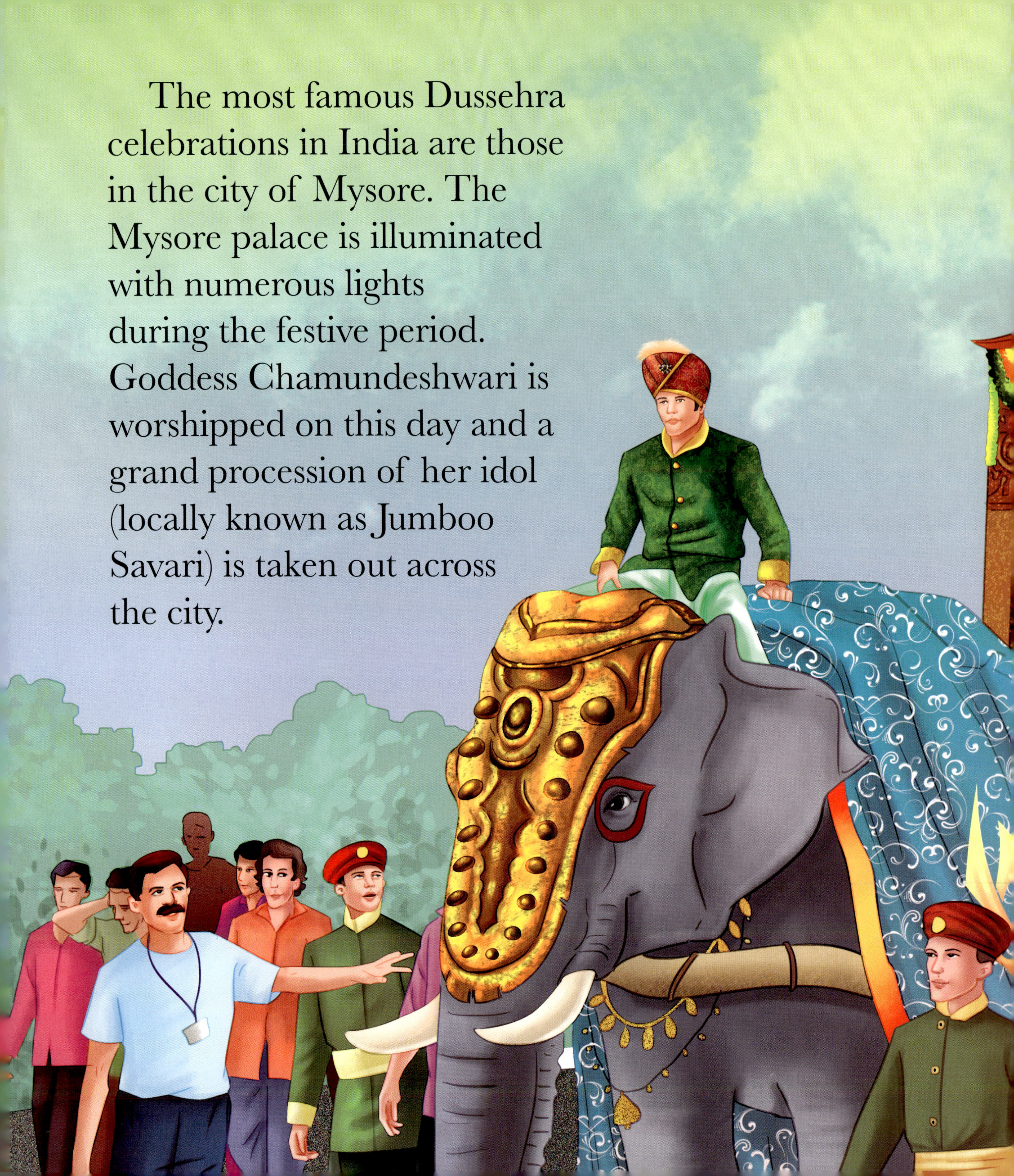

Dasara festival, as referred to by the people of Mysore, ends with the Panjina Kavayatthu, the torch-light parade. It is held on a grand note in the outskirts of the city.

People visit the pooja pandals wearing new clothes, prepare traditional food at home and celebrate the festival with their friends and families. This is how the festival of Dussehra is celebrated with great pomp and show, in different ways, throughout the country.